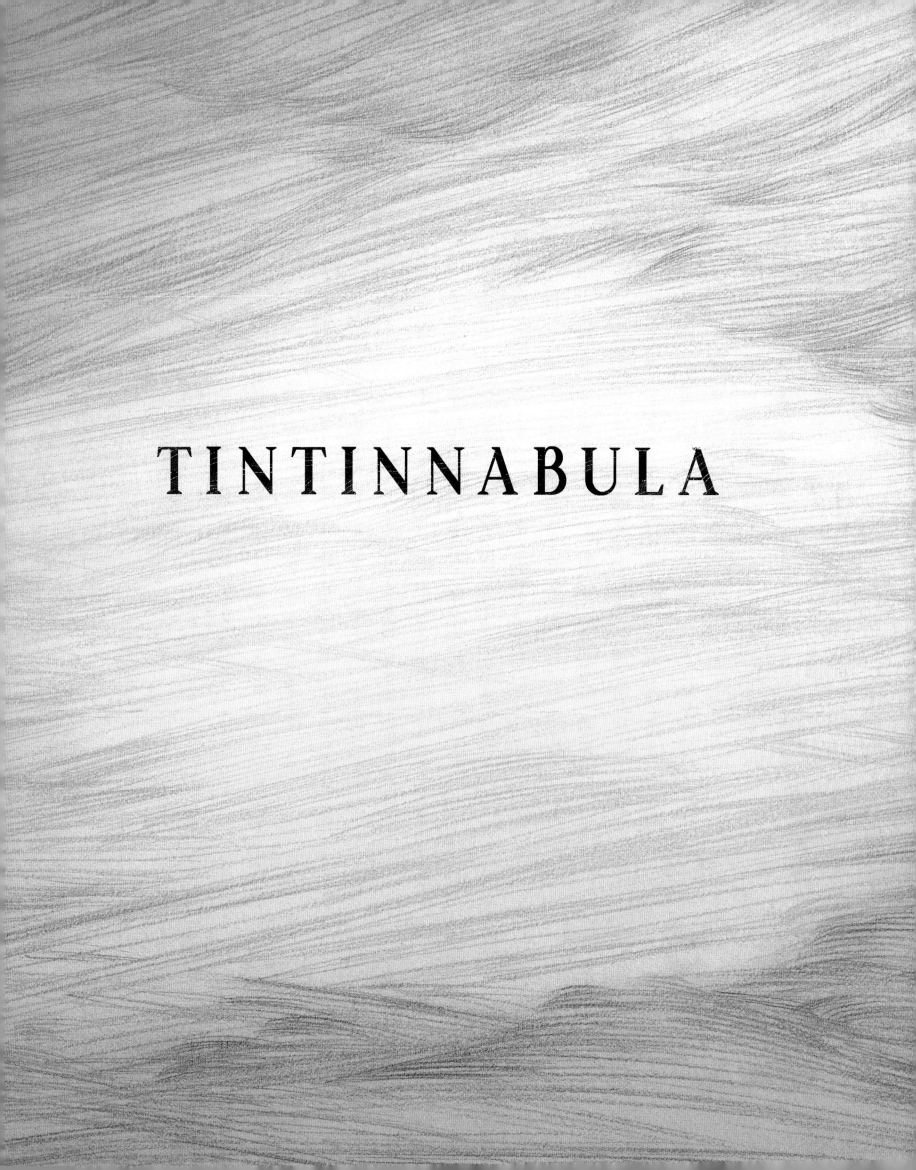

TINTINNABULA

For war children everywhere—ML
For my parents and all my teachers—RC

Little Hare Books
an imprint of
Hardie Grant Egmont
Ground Floor, Building 1, 658 Church Street
Richmond, Victoria 3121, Australia

www.littleharebooks.com

First published 2017
Reprinted 2018 (twice)

Cataloguing-in-Publication details are available
from the National Library of Australia

978 1 742975 25 2 (hbk.)

This book was edited by Margrete Lamond and Alyson O'Brien
Production management by Sally Davis
Designed by Hannah Janzen
Produced by Pica Digital, Singapore
Printed through Asia Pacific Offset
Printed in Shenzhen, Guangdong Province, China

7 6 5 4 3

The illustrations in this book were created with pencil and coloured digitally in Photoshop.

TINTINNABULA
MARGO LANAGAN

ILLUSTRATED BY ROVINA CAI

LITTLE HARE
www.littleharebooks.com

In times of drought and wind, in times of noise,
and stress and argument,
in times of ill feeling
and in times of fear,

from the bright bare ugly difficult
sweating sun-hot world I go
to Tintinnabula,

where soft rains fall.

Soft rains fall and silver, in Tintinnabula.
Soft bells ring and sweetly,
distantly, melancholically.

Hills rise and fall like breathing,
Green, breathing, grassy hills
rise—sometimes crowned with trees (dark)—and fall.

In Tintinnabula there are no others, no itches,
no irritations and no angers (silver rains
fall constant but not cold,
but cool and cooling only, calming).

There, I am not too big, too small for anything,
too weak, too strong. And I am never hungry;
I am never sorry.

In Tintinnabula,

I walk and I am always going somewhere.
Somewhere good is always
just beyond that breathing hill, and I
am walking there, through silver rains and under
silver clouds, brimful of light and water.

Who rings those bells? Who waits
in that good place beyond that rising,
falling hill? Who sings among those trees?

It's my own self who rings and waits and sings.
Myself all calmly, coolly comes to meet me,
walks towards me, through the silver rains …

of Tintinnabula.